DATE DUE

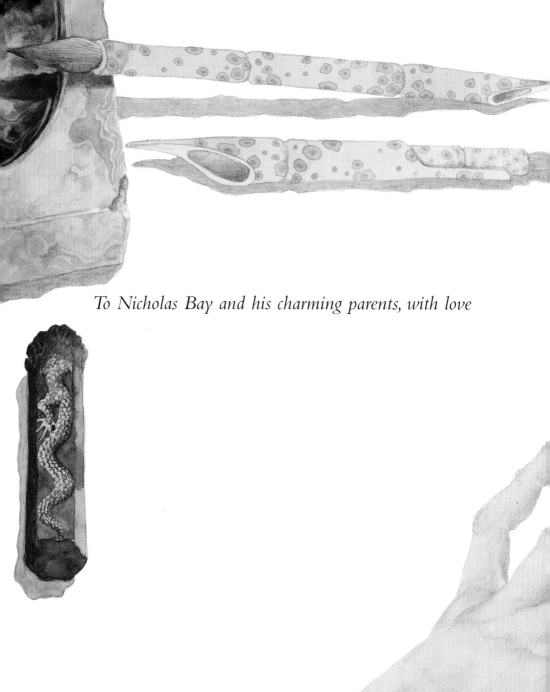

To Nicholas Bay and his charming parents, with love

Isaac Bashevis Singer

THE TOPSY-TURVY EMPEROR OF CHINA

Pictures by
Julian Jusim

Translated from the
Yiddish by the author
and Elizabeth Shub

A Sunburst Book
Farrar, Straus and Giroux

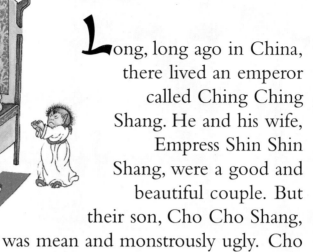

Long, long ago in China, there lived an emperor called Ching Ching Shang. He and his wife, Empress Shin Shin Shang, were a good and beautiful couple. But their son, Cho Cho Shang, was mean and monstrously ugly. Cho Cho Shang had a nose like a bulldog, lips like the snout of a pig, a low forehead like an ape, and the long ears of an ass. He had practically no neck, and his head sat on his shoulders like a snowman's.

When Cho Cho Shang grew up and saw in the mirror how repulsive he was, it made him furious. Instead of trying to acquire spiritual beauty and wisdom, which are more important than physical grace, he was filled with hatred and envy. But what could he do? At last a plan began to take shape in Cho Cho Shang's evil mind. Yes, he thought, there was something he could do, although not as long as his parents lived.

The old Emperor finally died, and soon after so did the Empress. Cho Cho Shang became the sole ruler of China.

It was the custom of the emperor to appoint a new cabinet, chosen from among the highest

mandarins of the court. For his cabinet, instead of picking the noblest and wisest of these lords, Cho Cho Shang searched for and selected the meanest men in China.

For three days and three nights the Emperor and his cabinet held secret council. On the fourth day the Emperor issued the following decree:

> *Attention! Be it understood that from this day forward everything called just and beautiful is declared unjust and ugly and everything that is considered mean and hideous is declared fair and lovely.*

The handsomest and most noble man in China was now, of course, Cho Cho Shang.

Cho Cho Shang selected his Empress according to the new taste. She was as ugly and coarse as her husband. But according to the new order, the Empress was the most attractive woman in the land.

Emperor Cho Cho Shang and his mandarins turned everything in China topsy-turvy. All the talented actresses were dismissed from the the-

aters and replaced by creatures who couldn't act. Since neither the Emperor nor the Empress could sing, a law was passed that all opera singers must caw like crows and grunt like pigs. And because both the Emperor and the Empress refused to study and could neither read nor write, it was announced that only the ignorant could become schoolmasters. In school the children were instructed to be lazy and dirty, to insult their parents and bully those younger than themselves. They were even praised for being insolent to their teachers. It became an accepted belief that only children who behaved in this manner would grow up to be citizens loyal to Cho Cho Shang.

Students were taught that facts were not of value in science. The job of the scientist was to invent complicated words and fancy names. There was no higher praise for a scholar than that his work was so deep he could not understand it himself. The scribes were ordered to use the most complicated characters. The more difficult the books were to read, the more profound they were considered to be. The libraries of China were soon filled with manuscripts no one cared to read.

At first the people of China openly mocked Cho Cho Shang's laws. But when those who made fun of the changed order were tortured and hanged, most people became frightened and pretended to agree with the upside-down state of things. After a meaningless lecture by one of the professors, the students would exclaim: "How clever he is!" If anyone dared to say that the professor was ignorant, he was imprisoned. That year the science award went to a mathematics professor who, through perverted logic, had proved that two and two are five. In poetry, a prize was presented to the poet whose verses made readers yawn and fall asleep in the shortest time.

Cho Cho Shang also decreed new table manners and fashions. Chopsticks were abolished and people were told to eat with their hands. When one was drinking soup it was proper to make a noise like a hog gobbling slops. The ladies were forced to discard their broad-sleeved, soft-hued silk robes and trousers. Instead, they had to dress in ill-cut glaring-colored rags. It was fashionable to adorn their hair, which they dyed green, blue, and purple, with living worms and frogs. Their eyebrows were plucked out entirely, and their nails were painted black. The most fashionable women shaved half their heads. Some men shaved half their beards.

When friends met in the street, they no longer bowed to each other as formerly, but tweaked each other's noses and said: "How unpleasant to see you this dreary morning. I hope never to see you again."

When visiting the sick, friends and relatives said to the patient: "Many people have died of your illness. I hope you do too."

Skunks were imported from faraway countries, and their stench was proclaimed the most precious perfume. It became the custom to dance at funerals and mourn at weddings, and for the poor to give charity to the rich. Books and articles were written on such topics as how to betray friends, break agreements, bear false witness.

Love was banned. The government told the people whom to marry and when. Often the bride and groom had to be chained and dragged to their wedding.

The citizens of the new China could do almost nothing without paying a tax. If one had mice in the house, one had to pay a special mouse tax.

As to the temples, they were no longer places to worship God and the souls of the fathers. Monkeys became the gods of the new China. The people were ordered to pray to them, and  the gorilla became the most honored god of all. When pupils entered a classroom, it was the teacher who stood up. Thieves became policemen and the honest police were put in jail. In public places the old offered their seats to the young.

The desire to have everything opposite from before became a madness. An educator proposed a plan according to which parents were to go to school and children to stay at home. Some women decided to wear fur coats in the summer and bathing costumes in the winter. The court doctor announced that it was healthy to eat when thirsty

and drink when hungry. A mayor ordered the street-lamps lit in the morning and extinguished at night. Other mayors soon followed his enlightening example. The court jeweler had the most brilliant idea of all: He suggested that the Emperor wear his crown on his feet.

A Court of Injustice was established. Burglars, forgers, and swindlers became the judges. In a famous trial the lawyer pleaded: "Your Dishonor, my client, the distinguished bank robber, who has received the Royal Medal for Thievery, asks for the trial to be dismissed, on the ground that he is about to rob the Mint. I propose that the witnesses against him be imprisoned for the rest of their lives."

And the judge, who kept his bare feet on the table, banged his gavel and called: "Motion granted. The court is to receive its usual share of the loot."

Since the new Empress had abnormally tiny feet, the noble ladies crippled their feet to make them smaller. When a baby girl was born, her feet were tightly bound so that they would not grow.

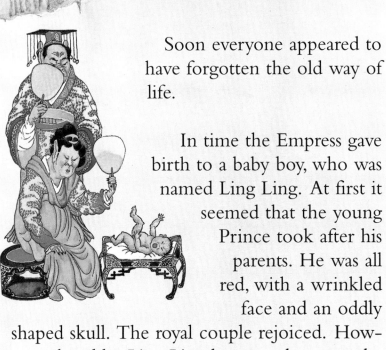

Soon everyone appeared to have forgotten the old way of life.

In time the Empress gave birth to a baby boy, who was named Ling Ling. At first it seemed that the young Prince took after his parents. He was all red, with a wrinkled face and an oddly shaped skull. The royal couple rejoiced. However, the older Ling Ling became, the more the Emperor and the Empress worried. His skin grew smooth, his skull round. He already had hair on his head. He had shapely hands and feet, and a delicate nose.

The news spread all over China that a freakish prince was growing up in the palace. Because all the people around him were different, the young Ling Ling began to feel uncomfortable. Often he lay awake at night and cried. His suffering made Ling Ling brood about matters that were forbidden in his father's kingdom. He began to question the rightness of things as they were. Word spread throughout the land

that the Emperor's son was not only hideous but a fool as well.

The Emperor had appointed tutors to educate his son in the new manner. He was taught painting, music, architecture, calligraphy, and astrology. Needless to say, in the arts, too, right had become wrong and wrong right. The master painters had been exiled and many of their pictures burned. The paintings sanctioned by the government consisted of smudges and smears. One sculptor became famous because he carved from cheese instead of marble. The music sounded like a door squeaking. Poetry was a mixture of words without rhythm or sense. The buildings had windows in the floors and the entrances were on the roofs. The ancient pagodas were torn down.

Prince Ling Ling tried to study, but somehow the arts did not appeal to him. He spent much of his time wandering in the palace gardens. The Emperor had ordered that all the flowers in the gardens be uprooted and replaced by artificial ones. One day Ling Ling found a blooming rosebush in a distant nook that had been overlooked. He picked a rose and took it to his room. When the Emperor learned that a live flower had been found in his son's room, he scolded him soundly. "How do you dare to bring the stench of a rose into my palace? All of China is laughing at you. How will you ever learn to rule our great nation?"

The young Prince said nothing. He had already discovered that everything in his father's kingdom was the reverse of what it should be.

But neither truth nor the feeling for beauty can ever be annihilated. There were still people in China who could not be fooled by the Emperor's commands. One of them was called Chung Mi Pu.

He was in charge of the royal museum in the Emperor's palace. Outwardly it appeared as if Chung Mi Pu complied with the Emperor's taste. He had all the masterpieces removed from the museum and replaced with the works of the Emperor's favorite artists. But Chung Mi Pu had not permitted the destruction of the old royal paintings. Instead, he had hidden them deep in the dungeons of the palace.

Chung Mi Pu was a widower. His wife had been a well-known beauty. Their small daughter, Min Lu, was five years old when her mother died.

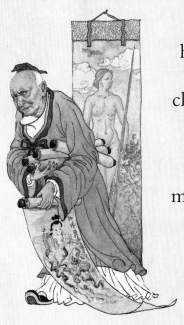

Min Lu was as charming as her mother had been. When it was decreed that all girl children be made to resemble the Empress and have their feet crippled, Chung Mi Pu did not have the heart to mar the girl's limbs. He made it known that Min Lu was very sick, and in a few days announced that she had died. Chung Mi Pu placed one of his daughter's dolls in a coffin and buried it in the family plot. Then he moved Min Lu to a dungeon apartment he had prepared for her not far from where the great paintings were hidden. Each day he himself brought her food and water and whatever else she might need. It was a secret he shared with no one.

In time Chung Mi Pu began to notice that the Crown Prince was not satisfied with the way things were. Ling Ling often asked him questions that others had refused to answer. The boy had a feeling for true beauty and justice that none of his tutors had been able to destroy. Soon his trust in Ling Ling became so great that Chung Mi Pu showed the young Prince the paintings and scrolls he had hidden away. He also brought Ling Ling to visit Min Lu.

By decree, all girls under sixteen had to have their heads shaved except for one pigtail in the center of their skulls. Their feet were bound and they all limped. And because they could not walk much, most of them became fat from idleness. But Min Lu had long black hair. She was slim and wore sandals that did not hamper her movements. Her father had taught her how to read and write and play the lyre. When Ling Ling visited her for the first time, he found her sitting, brush in hand, painting characters on rice paper. He fell in love with her the moment he saw her, even though love was strictly forbidden.

His mandarins made the Emperor believe that the people of China were exceedingly contented with his rule. But the opposite was true. Life in China had become unbearable. All over the land people were disgusted with the cruel laws, the pampering of criminals, the cult of ugliness, and the worship of the god-monkeys.

Every day Chung Mi Pu risked his life by trying to contact those who yearned for justice and beauty. At last he found a way to make the Emperor and his mandarins help him without their realizing it. He persuaded them that it would be an excellent lesson for the new generation to compare the great artistic achievements of the Cho Cho Shang era with the inferior art of former times. He told the Emperor he had discovered some paintings that by mistake had not been burned and could be used for this purpose. The Emperor and his courtiers were too busy drinking and gambling to care much about art. They permitted Chung Mi Pu to establish a new museum. In it he ordered the masterpieces of old China hung, together with the new paintings. Chung Mi Pu gave lectures comparing the two kinds of art for the museum's visitors. It appeared that he was delighted with the artists who adjusted themselves to the new regime and despised the masters of old. He would say with a twinkle in his eye: "Look for yourselves. Here is a picture of a garden. Some trees, flowers, birds, a pond, swans. It is true that they are all well painted, but who, nowadays, cares about old-fashioned nature? We are sick and tired of it. Long live our Emperor Cho Cho Shang, who ordered the burning of paintings like these.

"But now, citizens, look carefully at the pictures on the opposite wall. To the untrained eye they may seem to be just smudges, without any form, sense, or charm. But there is deep meaning in these blotches. They express perfectly the China of our dear Emperor."

And Chung Mi Pu would point out:

"This portrait, done in cow dung, is our beloved Emperor, may he live a thousand years or more. His soul is reflected in it admirably.

"This sketch, in tar and mud, is our great Prime Minister Phew Phew.

"This picture was created by our High Monkey Yum Chi Ku. He stuck his divine paw into a mixture of refuse and slime and with one slap made this monumental piece of art. It will take our critics at least a hundred years to fully appreciate its depth."

Most of the audience understood that Chung Mi Pu was poking fun at the false artists. There was laughter and applause. One of the most enthusiastic listeners was always Prince Ling Ling. His laughter and applause were the loudest.

The Emperor and the Empress were delighted to learn that Prince Ling Ling had finally become interested both in his father's government and in his art. More and more, Prince Ling Ling began to take part in public life. In his speeches, as did Chung Mi Pu, he seemed to praise everything the Emperor had established. He would say:

"I know, citizens, that you are happy with my father's government, even though there is little to eat and a lot of murder and theft. We may not have enough rice for our children, but our arsenals are filled with swords, spears, and poisoned arrows. We will invade Japan, India, and Tibet, and liberate the people of Afghanistan. Of course, we will have to pay a high price in lives and suffering to make our neighbors as intelligent as we are. Most of you may never live to see the day of our glorious victory. Nevertheless, we know you will fight to your last drop of blood to spread the worship of our monkeys throughout the world, and to make my cherished father the most feared ruler of all time."

Almost everybody understood that Prince Ling Ling was mocking the reign of his father. But the Emperor, blinded by conceit, took it all seriously.

"At last," he said to his wife, "our son is bringing us joy and honor."

And the Empress replied: "When he invades Nepal and kills many old men, women, and children, he may even become a national hero."

But one cannot rule for long with terror. And so it did not take too long before a revolution broke out. By the time Cho Cho Shang discovered what was happening, his palace was surrounded.

The Emperor and the Secretary of False Promises were watching a cockfight when the rebels, secret followers of Chung Mi Pu, entered the royal chambers.

The Emperor was shouting: "Tear him to pieces, Red! Pluck out all his feathers! Let him bleed to death. I bet another million yen that Red wins!"

"Fight back, you white coward!" screamed the Secretary. "It is not too late to save yourself."

"It is too late!" one of the revolutionaries cried out.

The Emperor saw that it was indeed too late. He pleaded for his life. He offered the rebels bribes, and promised them jobs in the Ministry

of Corruption; but it was no use. Cho Cho Shang and the Secretary were promptly beheaded.

When the Empress received word that her beloved husband had been killed, instead of weeping she began to laugh, in accordance with the accepted custom. She laughed for three days without being able to stop. The court doctors prescribed juice of copper, the fat of a stone, the horns of a red crow. Nothing helped. At the end of the third day the Empress gave one last fierce laugh and died.

While all this was happening, Chung Mi Pu insisted that young Ling Ling remain in the royal dungeons. He was afraid that an overzealous rebel might decide to kill the heir to the throne. After things quieted down, Chung Mi Pu let it be known that the Crown Prince was alive and well. He also revealed how in the past years he had helped Ling Ling study Lao-tzu, Confucius, and the other wise men whose works had been banned, and that the Prince excelled in genuine mathematics, astronomy, and law. Word spread quickly that the Crown Prince had worked with Chung Mi Pu to fight his father's topsy-turvy rule. Ling Ling was soon crowned emperor.

An emperor must have an empress. Emperor Ling Ling chose Min Lu to be his wife, and there was rejoicing throughout the country. The date of the wedding was set according to the ancient Book of Changes. All China prepared for the celebrations. From the farthest reaches of the empire, delegations began to arrive bearing gifts for the royal couple.

The tyrant Emperor Cho Cho Shang had not succeeded in wiping out the art of China. Hiding in caves, cellars, and attic rooms, talented artists, musicians, and writers had continued to paint, sculpt, compose music, and write in their own free way. The royal couple received precious scrolls, and statues cast in gold and silver or carved in jade and ivory.

The day of the wedding was declared a holiday. Gongs clanged, drummers beat their deerskin drums, and the sound of horns filled the air. Everybody flew kites. Processions carried paper dragons, banners, and torches. Masked magicians entertained the populace with their tricks. Marionette theaters throughout the country enacted the royal wedding.

All of China was one huge carnival. At night fireworks lit up the sky. All those who were fortunate enough to catch a glimpse of the royal couple in their wedding garments agreed that never had they seen a more splendid picture of youthful love.

The young Emperor immediately set about changing things. He appointed a new cabinet chosen from among the noblest and wisest of the exiled mandarins. Ling Ling's Prime Minister was none other than his teacher, Chung Mi Pu. Ling Ling drove from the court the ignorant, the flatterers, and the intriguers. The innocent were freed from prison and the thieves were again placed behind bars. The god-monkeys were banned from

the temples and returned to the forests, where they belonged.

All the ridiculous styles and customs of Cho Cho Shang's regime were abolished. Ling Ling ordered that roses, lilies, and all the other flowers be replanted in the palace gardens and public parks. In the schools and academies, reading, writing, mathematics, astronomy, and the wisdom of the sages were again taught. In time Ling Ling had many of the damaged pagodas and temples restored, and magnificent new ones built.

Alas, evil, too, cannot be rooted out by decree. Some customs of the time of Cho Cho Shang remained. The new Emperor could not convince the idle ladies of China that normal feet were more beautiful than bound ones. Besides, not everything the Chinese had inherited from former times was good. Emperor Ling Ling had to fight for fair government all his life, and his wife, Empress Min Lu, helped him. She bore him four daughters and three sons, and they were carefully educated to appreciate justice and love the arts.

Emperor Ling Ling lived in peace with all the neighboring countries and died at a ripe old age. His eldest son became emperor after him.

Nothing lasts forever. After generations, China again had some rulers who in their turn tried to follow the example of the wicked Cho Cho Shang. They, too, declared that wrong was right and that ugliness was beauty. However, their reigns did not last long either. The struggle between good and evil, beauty and ugliness is older than even China itself.

Text copyright © 1971 by Isaac Bashevis Singer
Pictures copyright © 1993 by Carl Hanser Verlag
All rights reserved
First American edition published by Harper & Row Publishers, 1971
First published with pictures by Julian Jusim in Germany by Carl Hanser Verlag, 1993
Printed in the United States of America
Typography by Caitlin Martin
First American edition, 1996
Sunburst edition, 1996

Library of Congress Cataloging-in-Publication Data
Singer, Isaac Bashevis, 1904-1991
The topsy-turvy Emperor of China / pictures by Julian Jusim; translated from the
Yiddish by the author and Elizabeth Shub.
p.   cm.
[1. Fairy tales.] I. Jusim, Julian, ill. II. Shub, Elizabeth. III. Title.
PZ8.S3574To   1996   [Fic]—dc20   95-44127 CIP AC